Life's a Bus
"Ride of Lessons"

Jonathan Dixon

Strap Up!

Key Contents

Contents

Intro

Upon reading this short story book, there will be a wide range of topics that will be addressed on this bus ride. Lessons that we all might encounter at some point in our lives and situations that we all could possibly face in today's world. Topics including insecurities, greed, friends, social media, and many more important topics.

The goal in writing this book was to touch not just one group of audiences, but a wide range of different audiences. The overall objective of writing this book was to show that there is a life lesson in everything we endure over our lifetime. Understand that some lessons are good, and some are bad; but there will be a lesson to be learned. I wanted these lessons to be short but powerful at the same time.

Understand some obstacles you might go through, you will never understand why, while some obstacles you face might help you evolve as the best individual you can be. After reading this story, I want my readers to realize that every day is a new day for you to change any situation. Now in this story, I will show you how our lives can resemble an object as simple as a bus; Understand this ride can go a little fast and get a bit rocky, so please "keep up" enjoy the ride!

Fight Adversity...

Bus expectations and maintenance on the BUS

This bus ride already begins when we were born and the expectations that follow our birth. Some buses start off expecting to go the entire ride with no casualties, no accidents, and no pit stops. On this journey you are about to take, the casualties are the people you hurt, the accidents being the mistakes you've made, and the pit stops are the breaks you would need to take from this crazy journey "you" are about to embark on. Wait, I can't keep going without letting you know what this bus resembles. Isn't that what the entire story is about? Well, in this story, this bus will resemble your life.

As we know, some buses start off needing a lot of maintenance having to be done from front to back before pulling off while others start their journey off with a brand-new bus and a touch of sunshine. I know the question you're asking - how can a new bus start off needing maintenance? Well, stop asking that question because, in life, you don't get to choose what conditions your bus will start with when "your" journey begins.

Understand that I will be assisting you on this long journey that you are about to embark on to the best of my abilities and not to worry, at the end, I will let you know "who I am". For now, let's get ready for this ride.

Now, on this journey, I will be teaching you what we call "life lessons." I will also be using some street terms with you, so just try to keep up.

Quick!

Swerve right, there's a pothole.

Understand for your journey, you will not be starting off with a brand-new bus neither will you have the best weather. Now Unfortunately, some buses will also start their journey with a bus full of past demons that already came with their bus. As for your bus, as you can see you will start off with a few of them as well. I'm guessing probably your parents could have hit a few "potholes" and had some accidents that contributed to the condition of this bus you have now. Now some buses will get to ride off starting their journey with a brand-new bus fresh off the lot, which on the streets some might call it "privilege." I've seen privilege firsthand, so I understand the frustration of having a "used" bus.

Hey, look! That bus just pulled off with their windows down looking all shiny while my bus won't even start. What's going on? Why did I have to get this piece of junk?

Piece of Junk? This the beginning of your life. Now you hold on a second, don't get it confused. Your "previous owners" did the best they could with this bus you have now!

Hey, maybe their bus was **used** when they got it as well. Look On the streets, we call that a generational curse. Now understand that they had done the best maintenance they could have with this used bus before you got it. Okay!

Just keep turning that key this bus will turn on eventually. Look before I keep going, I should let you know that the previous owners will be labeled as your parents on this journey. So, listen when you get this bus there will be no excuse for you to destroy this bus. Let's understand that the bus that just pulled off in front of you looking all shiny and new with great weather doesn't always finish before this used bus you have now, Focus! You must fix this bus to get going. Now never once did you hear me say it was fair who got which bus - is life fair?

Expecting to go this entire ride with no casualties, accidents, or pit stops will feel impossible, man! These roads really look rocky for me. Oh yes, I forget to mention, the roads, in this message for you, will be your life's path.

Sheesh! Wait, this wind blowing this bus is crazy! Okay, let me warn you, this wind hitting the bus is what we call "Trials and Tribulations." How crazy is it that some people start off their journey with a brand-new bus, clean roads, and no wind?

My bus barely has the doors on it, this bus sucks! At this point, I can see you're frustrated with the bus you started off with. Now LISTEN to the word, "started off," because this is just the beginning and we have plenty of time. Now that you know which bus "you" started off with understand that this is just the beginning and you still have to **drive** this thing. Please, stay focus and pay attention on this ride! Now, let's start this bus up. Roll down the windows and start going. You've got some passengers to pick up and a job to do.

I'm sorry, I didn't think I had to explain who the passengers are in this story, but I'll tell you anyway. The passengers will be the different people that will come in and out of this bus ride which is your life. Now they will play a very crucial role on this entire ride, but we will get to that later.

Let's focus. We're on our way to pick up our first passenger, and the winds have slowed down a bit. Also, your bus isn't driving so bad; Actually, it's driving pretty well. This bus isn't looking so bad. Well for now!

That's perfect because you're on the way now to pick up your first passenger. Fix the windows and make sure the floors are clean – I see you forgot to do that. Just like life trying to start off "fast" when you haven't taken care of the simple things.

Just hurry and fix that window and ensure the floors don't look too bad for now. Keep going and look focus at all times on this journey. On the streets, we call that being professional. Sometimes it's all about looking like you got it together. Fake it till you make it, do you hear me? We will address that, get ready the first passenger is coming aboard.

Passengers Boarding

Remember that you are a beginner on this journey, and the conditions are not the best for you. Also, you do not know these passengers boarding your bus. Now, you will swear with everything that you "think" you know these beautiful passengers approaching this bus, unfortunately at some point you'll realize what kind of passenger lies within this bus. Let's also remember your bus and the condition that you started off with, has made this journey a bit rocky.

Now Some passengers understand that you're a beginner and will be taking full advantage of you on this ride. At some point, you will realize what's going on. Now, this lesson will be unfortunate, and usually, this comes early in the journey. Now at times, you will swear you know these passengers they have opened up to you and even allowed you to introduce yourself, they have already expressed how much they valued you as a driver and have "sworn" that they would never take advantage.

Well, they shouldn't, since they're your first rider of the day, right? I know you're thinking to yourself that it's not fair that your bus is already **"Not in the best Condition"**
Why would somebody come to take from your bus? Understand that in life, people will take advantage of the weak. We will get to that, so pay attention.

If only this was a perfect journey. But if you remember, at the beginning of this story, I told you this ride would not be fair; so, just keep riding. Wait! We haven't even picked up our first passenger and you are already going too fast for me, slow down, please! See kid at the beginning of this journey, I forgot to mention, there's no slowing this bus down. Unfortunately, we will call this lesson, "life keeps rolling." Yea, that's going to be a tough one to understand, but look, this bus just started moving so keep up kid. We have our first passenger!

Usually, this first passenger will set the tone for this long exciting bus journey. Now understand every bus won't start with the same passenger, but that's okay because I will be addressing all passengers on this trip. For some, this first passenger will set the tone of high energy and positivity when coming straight through the doors, expressing a kindness that will make the "inside" of this bus shine. I wish I can pump the breaks for you, but you're going to have to take this ride for yourself! Get ready to open the door.

First and Second Passenger

Hey, Look! That first passenger just zoomed to their seat. Hey, let's watch this first passenger. Pay attention. I know he's sitting down now, but still watch him. On this journey, people will wait until you're **relaxed** to jump out the door and not pay. You need to pay attention to this lesson. When passengers feel like they know you, that's when they will try to test your bus, so keep your eyes on that damn mirror. Understand you still must look ahead Kid; don't stare in that mirror for too long, you still must pay attention to the road ahead as well. Okay, I can see how this is going to be a problem for you already.

You see how you must pay attention to that passenger and watch the road; Just keep looking forward. We call that **trust** on the streets, now you're going to have to use that word trust plenty of times on this ride, you'll see. What you will learn over time is that some people don't value trust as your bus does, but when the time comes you will be able to just ride without checking that mirror because your passengers will be **limited**. Okay, you look lost, I see; look, as this ride goes on, you'll know which passengers to let on the bus due to your past experiences with other passengers.

We will call that lesson, 'learning from your mistakes.'

Hey, here's another passenger coming aboard. Now, I must warn you that this passenger looks a little dirty; actually, they have the same dirt that's on **your** bus. Now, don't you judge this passenger, you hear me? Damn, I can see you are. Don't you judge anybody that comes to this bus kid. You think that because they look dirty, they're not worth much? That's silly.

What you will notice on this journey is some passengers will look dirty and even stink, but they will come with the most knowledge and wisdom you could ever gain.

They may even assist you on this journey, but you won't listen, and you will let them off early because you think you're better than them based on their appearance. How dare you? Okay, we will call this "being judgmental." Wait one minute how dare you judge someone that comes on this bus with the same dirt you have on the outside of **your** bus. Sounds just like life doesn't it? People judging others' dirt when they have on the same dirt. I'm assuming we understand this dirt represents problems on this journey but I'm not about to go there with you; just let this second passenger on the bus.

Demons and Seat Belt

Wait, let's go back to what you said about these demons being on my bus before I got this

bus! So, you're telling me I have to drive this bus and deal with demons I didn't bring on this trip?
Who said you didn't bring them?

Listen you don't get to ask questions; we must focus on this ride. You'll never get the answer to a question when you "know" you don't want the truth.

That's a little deep; don't think too much about that; Look since I'm here with you on this ride, I'll explain a bit more. Quick swerve to the left; it's a huge pothole ahead.

Back to the lesson. What you will learn on this journey is that you have to accept the truth no matter how bad it hurts. As we take this ride there will be a lot of truth that you will have to accept that will hurt but you will **have** to accept everything that comes with this ride. Now listen, I never said the truth would be easy; not everyone accepts the truth and they're riding "great". I'll let you choose if you want to accept your truth or not. Listen, don't you **compare** your truths to other buses, okay? This is your bus - stop being nosey and pay attention to your bus only. In the beginning, I told you this is now your bus and you control the passengers and everything that you allow to happen inside this bus.

Speaking of demons, silly me! I started off this bus ride all wrong, by not telling you to put your seat belt on. Seat belt? Okay, I'll explain; they call that seatbelt the Bible in the streets. Your previous owner, well she did an excellent job at putting her seat belt on every day and leading by example with her seat belt on. Look she told you to put that damn seat belt on before you entered this journey, so reach across that shoulder and strap up; you're going to need that on this trip.

Now understand you can't **make** everybody on this bus put their seat belt on, you hear me! Now at times, you will forget to put on your seat belt but when you hit that pothole, you will put it on quicker than you took it off.

You'll notice on this journey most people think they can make it without that seat belt and Boom! There goes a pothole. Now at times, you will forget to put on your seat belt but when you hit that pothole you will put it back on quicker than you took it off. Hey, real quick, one more thing. Look down to your left, this bus came with a trash can. We would label that trash can as excuses for now. Keep that trash can over there, okay?

Third passengers (innocent Passenger)

Okay, look a few of those passengers that will take this journey with you will give you their hard-earned time and you will use them for your own "selfish" ways on this trip, you will also waist their **valuable** time. How dare you? Look on the streets; we call them innocent passengers? Yea those will be the innocent people you hurt on this ride. I didn't hurt anybody on this ride what are you talking about? I see you're a little confused kid okay!

Look kid you hurt these passengers by not letting them off at their stop, knowing that was their **destination**. You kept them along this ride, knowing they had a stop to make. This will not be a long-detailed lesson; let's just call that lesson being selfish.

Hey, next time why don't you pay attention to their stop! You're starting to get confused again; just understand in life, you don't hold on to someone knowing you have to let them off at their stop. In life we can be selfish to a point to not acknowledge that you can be in the way instead of helping someone. In life either you're helping or you're hurting be a purpose in someone's life or just let them off at their stop! Got it kid.?

I can't believe you really thought you were going to take this entire ride without hurting innocent passengers. Trust me, you will hurt some passengers along this journey and you're going to be too "selfish" to admit the wrong turns you have made. Trust me, you will make a few bad turns; we all have. Now look for your missed turns you will have to give that passenger a refund because you made them miss their stop.

On this journey, a refund will resemble an apology. Now, most times when a bus makes a **bad** turn, they don't want to give their passengers a refund. How dare they? On the streets, we call that having too much "pride". Listen that word pride will destroy many relationships with your passengers. Don't be "cheap" on this trip, give them their refund!

Man Up

Hey! Let that window up! This wind is starting to pick back up a bit. I see you're trying to let a few of those demons out, but you'll see that some of them have an all-day pass so close that damn window. All-day pass? Yea, your previous owner well she had to take care of your bus by herself and did the best she could. But now, you're fighting with the demons of having to teach yourself how to survive on this road. Let's call this lesson teaching yourself how to become a man!

Now understand that there are other busses on this journey that have both their owners on their ride, teaching them along the way.

Unfortunately, you won't get that same treatment on this journey. I see you're confused. I'll break it down just a little more for you kid. That bus had what we call an extra assistant.

Okay look, on the streets, they call it "father." Hey, I'm sorry, I see you're a little disappointed. "That's not fair was my bus not good enough for him? Why cant I have both of my owners? I guess my bus was too dirty for him." Wait a second kid, that's not true; maybe his bus came with a few more **demons** than your bus did. Now, look, your previous owner, she did an excellent job and she took good care of your bus the best way she could.

Now she only could give your bus what we call guidance and principals, but you will need your other owner to help you become **tough** to take on all these damn potholes and terrible road conditions out here. I see you're a little scared. Look, you can still be tough and survive these roads; you just have to teach yourself. It's okay, relax, and just breathe. I didn't want to let you know at the beginning that you wouldn't have another assistant helping you on this journey. Hey, look at me. Focus! I don't want you dwelling on what you **didn't** have in the beginning. No excuses, remember?

Okay, this lesson comes with another rule: it's not how we get on this road but it's how we finish this journey. I'm sure you've heard that one before. Trust me, I understand your frustration. I won't judge you at all on this ride. My bus has had a few loose end along these roads also.

I've even tried to hide a few of them under a few innocent passengers. So, trust me, I understand. I guess self-medicating only covers up temporary pain, but hey, this is about your bus, mine is still on the road. Let's just pay attention to yours.

Hey, watch out! There's a pothole on the left. That was a close one kid!

Fourth Passenger

This passenger looks familiar, and you will swear that you know them from somewhere. Trust me, you don't but the connection is just so strong that you will just automatically trust them. You've trusted them enough to close your doors and start to pull off. See, on the streets, that's called "letting your guard down." There goes that concept of trust again. Sheesh!

Now understand that you and this passenger had a few things in common which "ignited" this strong connection that you're feeling. I know it's a great feeling, but that same feeling can also turn to regret and pain; you'll see, just keep driving. Hey, watch out! You almost hit another bus! Get it together kid! Okay, back to this fourth passenger.

Over time, they will have developed into a great passenger and this will turn into an extreme connection that will boost the entire atmosphere to the point where the inside of this bus will become brighter and actually make this trip a bit easier. We will call this passenger "close friends and family." Friends and Family? Yea, unfortunately, some of them will be leaving this journey early as well.

So why would close friends or family be leaving this journey early? Well, on this journey, even the ones you love won't understand the **final destination**. How can that be when that passenger is a close friend or family member? You think titles matter on this journey. Hey, it's not your fault they didn't want to go through the tough conditions with you. They will regret that later down this ride. Now here comes that hurt feeling, I know, just grip the steering wheel harder, it'll be okay.

Let's just mark this as another lesson. Look For now, you will let them ride, you hear me? You still have plenty of time to waste with them on this journey. Now they won't be worried about the time they take from you because they're going to come with their own motives. You see, the motives will be that black bag in their hand; it's a black bag, its dark so you can't see what's in it. Let's call this lesson, "Watch Passengers with the black bag."

Now Of course, there are several items in that black bag. These items are different but very powerful and will affect the entire atmosphere on the bus in a very bad way. Look those are some dangerous items in that bag. Items with the labels 'jealousy,' 'Envy,' 'Hate' or even worse, they might just bring their own demons with them; so, make room on this bus.

With these passengers, your trust will be growing over time because your guard is **down**. Now unfortunately as your trust begins to grow, their items in that bag will grow as well. These passengers can be tricky, and they have the potential to ruin this entire ride if you're not careful. Listen, you're going to have to drop them off real soon! Now look on the flip side kid there will be passengers that will be very supportive over this journey for you and even give you the **last dollar** they have to put in the gas tank to keep this journey going.

Listen kid, when you find that passenger, you don't let them off this bus, Understand me? This passenger will be what we call your support system in the streets. Now don't you allow that **one bad** passenger to affect the relationship you have with that great passenger you just let on your bus. Misery loves company, but we'll get to that later.

The Older Buses the Bad and Good

Hey, listen, I never said you were the only bus out here, there are other buses out here as well. They're a little older and what we call "seasoned buses." Those buses were once driving those same terrible wicked roads you're on. They even had the same misleading passengers you once had on your bus. Now you would think that you can relate to this bus and get some directions from this seasoned bus? Wrong! You're so busy focusing on the bad roads and different passengers that you're

"missing" the directions they're trying to give you.
Sheesh! Another lesson coming in.

This lesson is called "listen to
those seasoned buses!" Ok, I don't think you
understand, so I'll keep it simple - listen to your
elders along this journey! You could have avoided
so many of those potholes and terrible conditions
but see your hitting the same potholes they told
you not to run over. How about next time, just
listen and take the damn directions. How bout we
will call this "being stubborn."

I'm still not done talking about these older
buses on these roads. Now some of these older
buses want to take over your road because they see
you had an easier road and better bus than them.
Listen they will try to give you the **wrong
directions** and discourage you at times on this
journey! Don't worry, they're driving their
bus hating the journey they're currently riding on.
I'm guessing they didn't "take" the directions from
another bus when they were young like you did.
Now some older buses will be upset and try to
knock you off your journey, how about we call that
"misleading the youth."

Do you see the pattern now kid? See at this
point you have to ask what type of bus you want to
be at the end of this journey - a bus that tries to run

the new buses off the road or a bus that's trying to pave a better road for the new buses. Look, even though they're ahead of you on the journey, they still seem unhappy on their journey.

Why would they want the inside of my bus to be dark like theirs? Okay kid let's just call this "misery loves company." Don't ever be **afraid** to take the journey that makes you happy. As long as the journey you take is safe, just keep going. Don't take directions from every older bus just be aware of the wrong older bus you hear me?

Soul Ties

Hey, pay attention, you almost crashed over there looking at that bus. You think that the bus is pretty, don't you? Listen, that bus is to be respected she's rear and delicate; Don't be over there looking all crazy at that bus. Since I'm an old-timer, I'll let you in on a little secret you can park by any bus just don't let your passengers get **on her bus.** Hey, I won't go too far into details; we will keep this a PG13 bus ride for now. Listen, this is a major lesson you are about to take on and this could change your life forever; we will call this lesson "a soul tie."

This Lesson is no joke, do you hear me? If you park next to her bus and let your passengers on her bus, you could destroy her entire ride. I know you can't be that selfish. Can you? Damn, I forgot you are still at the **beginning** of this journey I can already see that you're going to pull around and allow them to get on her bus, aren't you? Don't answer, I would call you selfish, but I made that same decision on this same road kid.
Hey, you missed that stop sign you really keep looking at that bus. Focus on this road and pay attention.

You already have to pay attention to these terrible roads and deal with these conditions and you think you can just pull up next to another bus. I guess that's another lesson to be learned. Let's just call this "not having your priorities together." Silly Kid! Let's just leave it there. You'll learn what priorities are later in life, just keep driving. Listen when you start off on this journey, you're going to want to experience every pretty bus you see that's cool and everything until you **destroy** a bus so bad that you would want to pull over your bus and express care for her bus.

At this point, it's too "late". See, most buses will come and destroy her entire bus and expect her to understand while his bus pulls off leaving hers in need of repair. Do you think she should understand? You almost destroyed her entire ride. I wouldn't blame her if she didn't ever want to see your bus again. Listen here you be careful pulling up next to these buses because some soul ties don't go away.

Tires (Faith) and Steering Wheel (Hurt)

See, I forgot to tell you when you got this bus that these tires weren't the most stable, so with the roads being bad, terrible winds and wore down tires will now make this ride get a bit rockier. I'm sorry. I can't keep doing this; I never told you what the tires resemble in this journey.

They will be what we call 'Faith.' With all these bad roads and terrible conditions, your tires will also be tested early. Now Understand **New** tires won't be easy to come by along this trip, so you have to take care of these tires. Okay look; as you can see, you're going to be shaking up on this ride with these bad tires so some of those passengers that just got on will be leaving soon.

I can see this journey will be a little too rocky for them. Now you will understand later in this journey that you can't get **attached** to every passenger because they will be in and out of this bus. Unfortunately, I can see you will get attached! Look kid! I told you some of these passengers would be extremely close to you so when they do leave, it will feel like they took something from you.

Hey, I didn't say that passenger leaving would be easy but listen, grab that first aid kit and put that bandage over your steering wheel.

As you can see that steering wheel will be your heart on this journey. Hey, turn left, there is construction ahead! I see your steering wheel looked a little stiff on that turn.

Understand that on this journey, your steering wheel will pull you in **several directions**. At times people will come up to the front of this bus and twist your steering wheel forcing you to pull over. Unfortunately, there would be no stopping, so you will have to deal with that hurting vibration on your steering wheel. Understand that the steering wheel controls everything on this bus inside and out. So, when that steering wheel stops working, everything stops on this journey. You must protect that steering wheel at all cost, understand?

Sheesh kid, I see your steering wheel is starting to get harder to steer and starting to lock up now. How about we call this lesson you're experiencing "getting hurt." Look, your faith in your passengers and the faith in your bus will be challenged. Just keep going and beat that red light! That last passenger must have taken a lot from you when you dropped them off, I'm guessing.

Hey, back to that lesson we talked about earlier; remember it was called 'man up'! Now look; your faith on this journey will be challenged. Just keep going and beat that yellow light!

Significant Other

I see you keep looking in the rear mirror, looking at that passenger, she must have caught your attention. I see. Listen that passenger has one of the kindest hearts that you will ever come across on this journey. I see you're gripping the wheel tighter, relax. That passenger you are staring at in that mirror will keep you going on this bus. They will motivate you along this journey and inspire you to push throughout all this craziness around you.

We call this passenger your significant other. Hey! Hey! You better focus on this road. Stop looking in that mirror so much. Now we've been riding this ride long enough for you to understand that the same passenger you were just mesmerized by can also be the complete opposite and bring their **own demons** as well with them on the bus. Unfortunately, some buses significant other can be the reason their journey doesn't reach its **full potential.**

Now I would hope on this journey you will be able to ride out with the passenger that won't have their own demons. Trust me, but Hey, there's a chance you might not be so lucky.

Now These different traits that this significant other can bring are ugly and can go by the names 'selfish,' 'controlling,' 'abusive,' and don't forget that little demon they call 'sneaky,' hiding behind them. That little bastard! Okay, I see you look disappointed again. Let me ask you this question, how do you expect someone with their own demons to support and love your bus to the fullest?

Quick! Look in the mirror, you notice that they're battling with a few demons on this journey as well. I won't get too deep into this lesson. Let's just call this lesson "trying to force toxic relationships." Let's hope you get the passenger that's willing to support your dreams and aspirations on this journey. You're a good kid so you should be okay, or maybe not. Make a stop at this corner!

The Law

Wait, what's that small white bus with the different color lights on top and chains dragging behind their bus? Hey, pay attention, you don't want that small white bus with the different lights on top to see you not paying attention to the road. Look at me! Those small buses with the lights at the top; we call that the 'law on the streets.' You have to be careful on this journey at times those small buses with the lights on top will pull behind you and tell you to pull this bus over so they can search this bus for absolutely no reason. They might even make a few of your passenger get off. Look on the streets they call this 'racial profiling.'

Let me tell you something; You must listen to these buses do you hear me! They will end this journey "forever" for you! I've seen that happen to a few casualties in my day. Hey, I didn't do anything wrong; Why would they harm my bus? Don't you see you have a **different** color bus from theirs? You looked, used, and beat up. your value means nothing to "some" of them, you hear me!

Wait this ride is really starting to become unfair. I just want to ride on my journey in peace. I have to watch out for other cars as well!

Hey, stay focus, Their driving behind Us...

Why does it matter if my bus looks different? Didn't I tell you kid what happens on this journey won't be fair? Listen, when those small busses approach you, you will open that door and turn off this bus. Do you hear me? Listen I don't want to hear about your bus ending its journey early on the radio; do you hear me? That's a little too much for you, I see.

It's okay; you just stay focus, you understand me? Okay, that's enough about those little small busses with the lights on top. Just keep staying focus. I don't want you to be on their radar. I hope you understand that lesson. It will be a life saver.

The Birds

Hey what's all these black birds around the bus? Listen, those birds can get into the view of the window if you let them. Now you will have to watch out for those birds. They are small but their chirp can be really loud. I want you to understand that they will be doing a lot of chirping at this bus, okay?

Now sometimes that chirping will annoy you to the point where you will feel as if you have to pull over. Man! Why are these birds chirping at my bus so much their pretty loud? Listen, don't pay these birds any attention. Okay, all that chirping you hear those birds doing; we call that 'negativity' on the streets. Quickly, this is a very valuable lesson, as you can see, the birds are on the outside of the bus and you're letting their chirp affect the inside of your bus.

Man! that chirp is really starting to get louder and louder. Look don't pay attention to those birds; Their mission is to throw you off your journey. Blow your horn; that might scare them off.

Listen; in life, you will have many people talking and giving their negative opinion while your bus is on this journey. What I want you to understand is that their on the outside of this bus, looking in. Okay, back to this journey, you cannot allow a little chirp to affect the entire atmosphere of this bus. The best way to get rid of those annoying birds is to keep going ahead; matter of fact, press the pedal harder. Let them chirp; just don't let them get in the way of your **view**. Stay Focus!

Look, you have to watch out for those birds. They are small but their chirp can be really loud. Now I want you to listen; they will be doing a lot of chirping at this bus, okay? Now, sometimes that chirping will annoy you to the point where you will feel as if you must pull over. Keep going! Why are all the birds flying together? Remember; kid misery loves company!

Gas and Insecurities

I see you keep looking at your bus in disgust. What's the matter? Okay, I get it; you think your bus is not worth much. I can tell by the way you drive this bus that you don't have the most confidence in your bus. We're going to call this lesson "insecurities."

Trust me, I understand that your bus being dirty and old makes you feel **worthless**, I see. Not only is your bus dirty, but you've already been through a lot on this journey so far. I see with all that you've been through your bus is now starting to get low on gas. Okay, for this journey, gas will resemble your confidence. Now I'm starting to see that everything you been through on this journey has made your gas low over time. Listen, you're going to have to still stay on this journey.

Eventually, you will be able to put more gas on this bus. Understand that you're not alone. There are a lot of buses driving around here low on gas too or just **hiding** their gas hand. Listen I'm going to teach you a key part of this lesson.

At this point, you can still take this journey with low gas on this bus you don't have to stop. Don't allow the fact that you're low on gas end this journey early.

Slowly, over time, you will have a full tank of gas but for now, you're going to have to coast this ride! In Life the **opportunities** and **experiences** you have should help boost the gas in this bus for you over time. You must be willing to get outside your **comfort zone** to help increase the gas in this bus understand me?

Now listen because your gas is low, don't expect other passengers to understand how this bus is running, you also can't expect your passengers to understand what's going on up here with your gas tank. How about we just call this lesson "stop expecting someone to love you if you don't love yourself." In life, you can't expect someone to see the value of your life when you don't even see it for yourself.

At times, your passengers will see more of the value of your bus than you do.

Some passengers will see around the dirt and just care about the inside of your bus Look You have to get it together soon kid.

Radio

Hey, turn that radio down. Radio? What is the thing you call Radio? Well, this radio will be a symbol of social media on this journey. Social media? Yea, this little radio keeps most of these buses going. Some buses can't even "function" without this radio and they live just to turn this radio on. This radio has made these buses live a **"fairytale"** journey out on these roads, so be careful. Fairytale journey? Yea. See, on this radio, a bus can **pretend** to be anything they want to be on this radio. Pretend?

What do you mean by pretend? Okay kid understand that a bus can come on this Radio and talk about how better their bus is compared to yours, when in real life, their bus looks just like yours, if not worse. Now in the street terms, we call this 'faking for social media.' Listen, don't you be on this radio pretending to be something you're not, because one day someone will see your bus and **noticed** you lied about what kind of bus you had on the radio! Yea, I'm sure you're thinking that can be very embarrassing.

Okay, so you're telling me another bus will come on this radio just to try to impress other buses that don't have nothing. My bus doesn't even have anything special why would they try to impress me? I guess they must be low on gas kid! I can see you're starting to catch on. Listen, this radio is no joke; this radio has destroyed plenty of buses. You must control this radio, okay? Destroyed? How can this little radio do so much damage to this big bus? That lesson will be called the power of social media!

Now listen here; don't be looking for approval from this radio; so many of these buses let this radio determine how the inside of their bus will feel. You're lying, that's crazy! First of all, I am not a liar, Now look; if you think that's crazy, turn to the next song and just ride. It's the same pretending on every station. Matter of fact let me see this radio. You need a break from this thing.

Your Own Kind (The Same Bus)

Hey, that bus next to me is trying to take over my lane and knock me off the road. Didn't I tell you to keep your head on a swivel? Why would that bus try to knock me off my path; we are on the same road and by the looks of it, we have the same bus? Listen this will be another tough lesson; even your own kind will try to knock you off the same road you are both on. Why we look just alike? Didn't I tell you that looks can be deceiving?

Understand that on these roads, sometimes, your own kind will be your biggest obstacle and threat. I can see that's going to be a little too street for you. I'm going to keep it simple for now; just watch every bus, even the ones that look like you. Yes, even buses that look just like you! Okay, this is crazy; I was minding my own business, and here comes that bus trying to knock me off my journey. Now you would think because you have so many similarities and have the **same** bus, you would stick together and help each other on this journey. Wrong! Remember that misery loves company we talked about this kid!

You're starting to look really upset, your temperature gauge is starting to rise, and your engine is getting hotter.

Look at me; you control that anger! Control my anger? You can't be serious; he almost tried to knock me off the road. Look, don't you think about crossing over there to that bus's lane! I will not let that rage you're feeling allow you to make a bad mistake on this journey.

See, remember those little white buses with the different color lights I was telling you about earlier; well, they will **expect** you to get what we call 'revenge' on the streets. They want you to get revenge so they can take your bus off this journey in those medal chains you seen dragging on the back of their bus. Understand that revenge and anger you're feeling towards that bus is what we call 'black on black violence' in the streets, and that needs to stop; you understand me?

Now look, I've seen enough of that in my day, okay! Listen, it's too many of us already in the Junkyard. You hear me? What is a junkyard? On the streets, we call that the grave. See, revenge will get you two places; either the junkyard or this big building to your left; look really quick. Why does that big building have those big gates around it?

Listen to me that building that has those huge gates around it is known as the 'prison' on the streets. Hurry Speed up; let's get far away from that building okay!

The Heat

It's really beginning to get hot in here! This is unbearable, hey can we please turn on this air conditioner? Silly! That air conditioner doesn't work and never has. This heat is no joke. Look, kid, I'm going to let you in on a little secret, okay. Just come closer I'm going to whisper this one to you. Well, this heat will represent **anxiety** on this journey.

Hey, why did you have to whisper that to me? Unfortunately, some passengers don't want others to know that secret as well. It's considered "embarrassing" out here on the streets and most buses like you don't understand it. You look disappointed. I'm sorry! What you're going to have to realize on this ride is that this heat will come and go and most times you can't control it. You mean to tell me this is my bus and I can't control my own heat? Listen, if you can't handle all this heat, grab that water bottle to your left.

What's this water bottle?

For this journey, this will be Alcohol. Understand This Alcohol will numb most of your problems on this journey, so drink up. Hey, slow down Kid! Now this will make the heat not feel as bad for now. Okay, that's enough; I'll drink the rest to take some of the heat off my bus. Now listen there are other passengers on this bus that have that same water bottle so it's okay; they're just **hiding** their water bottle in that bag with the secret motives.

Why does this water bottle make me feel so relaxed? It's okay Listen this lesson is called "hiding the pain." Trust me you would be using that water bottle for a lot more other things on this journey, I'll explain later. Now I will let you figure out how to pass this lesson because I'm still learning that one myself. Now understand this heat will turn on randomly at times but you're going to have to just grip that seat belt and keep driving, you hear me?

Okay, I can see you're going to be worried about this heat but understand you still have all of these passengers aboard and a long journey to finish. Don't worry, a few passengers are hot as well on this bus, so you're not alone, Quick look in the mirror there's a passenger behind you drinking their water bottle.

They must be hot as well.

Dark Clouds

What's this dark cloud above the bus? It's coming down real fast. Dark clouds? unfortunately, that cloud will represent depression on this journey. Wait, this looks bad; it's really starting to get close to this bus.

Hey, give me back that water bottle, man these clouds mixed with that heat feels unbearable. I understand how you feel. Push that pedal, and let's try to get past this dark cloud. Hey, Kid, slow the bus down you're going to fast now! I see you're really trying to get past this dark cloud.

So now you're going way too fast and you definitely need to start slowing down on that water bottle; it's starting to make this bus swerve. Listen it might make you feel relaxed, but it will also kill your vision! So, relax! Give me that water bottle! I see a little **light ahead**, keep going. Listen, unfortunately, just like the heat you won't be able to control these clouds, okay?

Now just like this heat, other passengers on this bus are under that same cloud as well. So, understand you can't expect them to get you through these clouds.

You're going to have to Man up, again! Damn man these dark clouds making everything around the bus look dark.. Focus! These clouds will ruin this entire journey if you don't get it together. When will these dark clouds go away? Unfortunately, Kid, I don't have the answer. If you stay focused and understand that these dark clouds are temporary, you will weather these clouds.

Sometimes these clouds can make you do the unforgettable, so press the pedal!

Now I notice you haven't grabbed that seat belt, and I see you're scared as hell, and you're not sure where this journey will end. Your tires are still worn down and everything around this bus is beginning to get dark. At this point in the journey, you will feel like this is the worst time, and the next day of happiness for you is hundreds of miles away. Look at me, Kid, you must realize the future of this journey can change tomorrow. This journey is never over.

I'm starting to notice on this journey that you will grab that water bottle quicker than you clutched that seat belt. You have no faith, I see. See, new tires are **very** expensive and hard to maintain and so is faith. You need to start believing in these tires soon or you will have to drink more water bottles than you could ever imagine.

Fix your Faith!

Ending this Trip Early

Hey, your bus is quiet, what's going on? You're not looking too good, and the lights on the inside of this bus have gotten low.

I can tell you have a tremendous amount of pain pouring out of this bus now. Hey, I hope you are not thinking about ending this journey early.

Look, I've been through so much on this journey and it's becoming overwhelming. My steering wheel can't take any more pain from this journey. This journey is taking a toll on me, and I'm not sure how much I can take!

That last passenger and what I've been through really took a lot out of me. I think I might just turn this bus off forever.

Hey, Snap out of it now! How dare you think about such a crazy thing! We call that the easy way out. You will stand firm and step on that pedal. Do you hear me? Understand once you end this journey, there's no coming back from that? On the streets, we call that being selfish.

There are people on this bus that depend on you. How can you think of such a thing? It's a long and hard journey, trust me, but you have to "push" the pedal to see what the journey looks like over these dark clouds and rigid roads. We have plenty of time on this journey; things will change, kid. At this point in the journey, you have to understand these passengers depend on you to finish this journey for them. Look, they might be under that same cloud and depending on your bus to get them out.

How would they feel if you ended this journey early? They'll be devastated! This lesson will be called "fighting to live another day." I see that the water bottle only could cover so much pain.

You can only mask the pain for so long until you have to embrace the truth head-on. Until then, your bus will just be on the run from all the realities that happen along these roads. Trust me, these roads will get better over time, and maybe one day your bus will have an upgrade as well. For now, we must keep going, put that seatbelt back on. Now, make this Left!

The Shiny New Bus

Hey, wait you never told me where that other new "nice" shiny bus drove off to at the beginning of the journey. Man, I can see you're nosey but hey, I use to be like that back in my days. Now I won't go into details of their life journey or their ride. This is about your bus, Okay, fine; I'll go into little details. As you can see that other bus sure had some great roads and everything new didn't it? Actually, if you take a look over to your left, that same bus is right next to you.

As you can see, your bus is on the same level as that "shiny" bus now. Actually, that bus looks a little dirty now; kind of look just like yours now! I see you're looking a little confused. I get it because that bus started off with everything "new" and the roads were perfect with sunshine, you figured that their bus would be way ahead of your bus still looking nice and shiny. See kid, that bus made too many pits stops, and used their trash can a lot. Okay, I'll go back just a little to earlier in the journey; let's remember trash can resembles excuses. Now even thou your bus was much different and had way "less" than their bus, you both still had the same type of passengers.

I guess they had more passengers with worse demons than you did. See, I get it; you thought because that bus had everything together that they didn't have any demons inside? Silly Kid! Well, how about this; we'll call this lesson, 'everything that glitters isn't gold.' Understand this journey is a marathon and you can burn out fast when you have **everything** new and the roads paved for you. Understand that sometimes when you have to go through worst conditions, at the beginning, you appreciate the victory more at the end, you hear me? Even though your bus has been through more winds and bad roads, you never once stopped.

Now "blow" your horn and wave as you pass the bus that was all nice and shiny in the beginning.

Bag Full of Money

Hey, look, one of your passengers left you a bag full of money! Hey, give me that bag. Fine, it's your bus, here's the bag! So, let me guess now you're going to buy a whole bunch of new stuff for this bus? Don't answer that I can already tell you are. Yes, I will be getting everything new on this "piece of junk" bus!

Piece of junk? It's funny how the Money is already making you look at the things that helped get you to this point differently now, that's funny! "Are you kidding me? I can finally buy everything new on this bus. I'm excited!" Trust me, I understand I upgraded my bus a few times back in my day. I can tell you're letting this money **change** you and the entire atmosphere of this bus. Slow down kid I want you to be careful with this current feeling.

On these streets, we call this feeling you have "greed." Hey, but wait you talked about all this new stuff you're getting for your bus but you didn't once mention what you were doing for the passengers that endured this crazy journey with you! Listen, I've seen this money change a few buses. Pay attention to me, don't you let this money change you, do you hear me? You almost forgot to **reward** the passengers who helped get you through those tough times along the journey. How about we call that mistake you made "forgetting where you came from."

It's Ok! Sometimes that can happen. Understand that money will make this bus do some crazy things. Wait, some passengers are beginning to **stare** at this bag full of money. Now, look at what you've just done! Now some of those passengers have seen this bag that's full of money. Quick, hide this bag now! Hey, why would I hide this bag of money? This is my bus! Well if the money changed you, what did you expect it would do to the passengers riding your bus? Some of these passengers are starting to look at you funny now since they've seen that bag of money. They will now start to ask for money to put in their bag. Hey! What if I don't want to give them my money? Are you kidding me?

Look not only would they be upset that you didn't give them some of the money but they will start to make you feel as if you never gave them a ride at all! On this journey, you will understand that it will never be enough for some passengers what you give them. We will call that lesson "not being able to buy love".

Hey, sometimes the money won't change you, but it will change the passengers around you. Quick, make this stop; they want to get out because you didn't share that money! This money is starting to cause a lot of problems for your bus, I see. It seems like you were a little happier before you received this bag of money. Fine, we will label the second part of this lesson "Money doesn't buy happiness." Turn left!

Passengers Leaving Early

Now, unfortunately, some passengers on this ride will be leaving you early not because they wanted to but because they suddenly ran out of "Time" along this journey. Now this will be one of the "Toughest" lessons to understand on this journey. See, I really don't want to talk about this one but I'm here to prepare you for everything, you hear me kid?

You're going to have to understand that some of those passengers that's close friends and family will, unfortunately, run out of time on this journey. This lesson will be called "handling death." Fine, here's the water bottle! Unfortunately, you're going to need that water bottle for this lesson.

I don't know what you're talking about but I will not have any close friends and family leave my Bus early. Look, I know it's tough and hard to understand, I can even see your bus is starting to get darker on the inside again. Trust me, I understand it will feel like a piece of you leaves when they leave, and your bus will lose some light on the inside. Hey look, I still have this bag full of money. Here, bring them back! Unfortunately, kid, money can't buy everything, and you have to appreciate every second you have with your passengers. This bag full of money **can't** buy time. I understand you were close to these passengers.

Close? That's my family and friends you're talking about, are you serious? Listen, I've had a few close friends run out of time and I couldn't understand why as well. I won't lie to you that the pain you're feeling through the inside of this bus will probably never stop, but at some point, it will become bearable enough for you to finish this journey at some point. Okay? Between you and me, I still don't know all the answers to what happens on this journey we take, but that's when you grab that seat belt and keep the inside of this bus as **bright** as possible so you can make it through this journey. Understand? We will call that lesson "fake it till you make it".

Sunshine

Hey, what's that Sun doing in my face? You told me it would just be wind, passengers, and a few cracks in the roads; I can't see right now. Hey, you better get used to this sunshine; that's your damn daughter. Hey, wait! This is starting to become a lot to handle. Look, this sunshine will be a new experience for you, and I can tell you're scared as hell right now. Now, remember your previous owner; she installed plenty of principles and guidance into your bus and you will use what she taught you to raise this child, do you understand me?

You will be here for your daughter no matter what it looks like on the inside or outside of this bus. By accomplishing this lesson, you will be breaking what we call a generational curse. You will be the best protector for this beautiful sunshine, and you will vow never to leave that beautiful sunshine you see in your windows.

Now she's going cost you most of that money that you received from that passenger, so get ready. Look you get that bag full of money ready, okay? Wait a minute this sunshine in my face keeps me going now and it's the most beautiful image to look at. Now I'm starting to feel this surge of energy from this sunshine this feels amazing, I feel alive! Hey, snap out of it that's good and all but these roads and wind is starting to pick back up. I'm sorry but this sunshine is beginning to change my mood for this ride, what is this feeling?

Hey, it's called being a Parent. Okay, this is a great feeling, but I have a question - how can I ride with this sunshine in my face while teaching myself how to handle these roads, watching these passengers and trying to handle this damn wind? Wait! I'm not ready for this trip can we take a pit stop I need to get a few things together. Didn't I tell you nobody will be taking a pit stop? You better keep going. Look, you'll be fine. You might want to grab that Seatbelt again.

The Rain (Past Trauma)

The sun is starting to fall a little It's not dark yet, but it's getting there. Look at that beautiful sunset. Now things are starting to cool down a bit. Now listen I want you to start slowing this bus down. At this point, we both understand you've had a few passengers in and out of this bus, and your journey has been filled with memories good and bad. Now, those directions that you have are finally reading a little clearer now. Hey, wait, what's that falling on my window?

Quick, turn on those windshield wipers. Hey, what is this? Well, this rain will represent regrets and past trauma. Now that your bus has slowed down, you're beginning to think about all the pain you have gone through over this long trip. I'm going to warn you now, this is a bad mistake that other buses make on their journey. Let's call this lesson "looking back in the past." Now some people on the streets may call this living with past trauma. This will be a very important lesson to learn but also understandably most buses will experience this throughout their journey.

At times, all that pain you went through will catch up to your bus, and all you will think about is the bad passengers that hurt you!

There you go, grabbing that damn water bottle. How about this for now, you will only worry about the end of this journey and not what happened in the past on these roads.

Why would you look back to times and passengers that hurt you on this journey? Don't you want to move forward? It's okay; I understand that can happen at times on this ride. Now let me ask you a question kid; how can your bus move forward when you're always looking in that mirror? Sometimes you will let passengers take too much from your bus when they leave. Don't you allow those bad passengers and bad times to affect your bus moving forward understand?

Trust me, the feeling of hurt that you experienced will make this bus take time to recover but at some point, you've got to take control of the bus. Look some buses hold on to so much pain that they miss many opportunities along their journey. Stay focused and press the pedal. I want you to turn those windshield wipers on and keep your vision clear for the rest of this journey. You almost let that rain stop you from reaching your full potential on this journey.

Hey, make a stop at this Light!

Last Ride

Okay; well, it looks like my time is up! Your time is up? What do you mean? Silly Kid! You do realize that on this entire trip, it's been you getting yourself through this entire journey. Now, you know I had to save the best one for last.

On the streets, we call this, 'your consciousness and self-motivation.' Now, as you can see, "you" had it in you the entire time. I've watched you go through plenty of pain, but I've also seen you meet some tremendous people that helped change the entire atmosphere on this bus. Now, understand that your journey is far from being over, and you still have to take care and watch over a few passengers on your journey. I want you to realize the worth that your bus holds on this journey now.

You have passengers that look up to you and expect you to finish this journey strong. You will be an example of a bus that had to endure trials and tribulation, and you made it through; so now, help others and lead by example. In the streets, we call this a '**Leader.**'

Hey, remember you will still have some potholes and a few bad winds on the way. From what I can see, you will be able to handle them. Always remember when it gets to bad and the tires start to get shaky again; grab that seatbelt. Just do me one favor kid and go slow on that water bottle for me. Sheesh; you can drink! Notice as this ride got longer, you might not have upgraded everything to the best on the outside, but the inside of this bus has changed the most.

When this journey is all over, they won't remember your bus for how fast you went, but for the impact this bus left on all your passengers along this journey. Now, for that sunshine in your window, she will be getting bigger and you have to give her everything that your bus didn't have. Don't you allow those other buses that were trying to get in your lane throw you off this journey; do you hear me? That sunshine is not worth you going to any junkyard or that building we passed having chains around them.

So, for me, I'm going to continue my journey, and hopefully, we will pass each other on these crazy roads in the future; but for now, my time is up!

Made in the USA
Monee, IL
27 February 2022